与子书

A Book For Gentlemen

徐新松 宋勤英 徐谦 ○ 著

经济日报出版社

图书在版编目（ＣＩＰ）数据

与子书 / 徐新松，宋勤英，徐谦著 . -- 北京：经济日报出版社，2022.9
ISBN 978-7-5196-1165-1

Ⅰ . ①与... Ⅱ . ①徐... ②宋… ③徐… Ⅲ . ①书信集—中国—当代②家庭教育 Ⅳ . ① I267.5 ② G78

中国版本图书馆 CIP 数据核字 (2022) 第 144391 号

与子书

作　　者：徐新松　宋勤英　徐谦
策划编辑：姜　楠
责任编辑：陈礼滟
助理编辑：李敏婧
责任校对：范立君
插画设计：莫那文化
封面设计：晴海国际文化
出版发行：经济日报出版社
地　　址：北京市西城区白纸坊东街 2 号 A 座综合楼 710（邮政编码 :100054）
电　　话：010-63567684（总编室）
　　　　　010-63584556（财经编辑部）
　　　　　010-63567687（企业与企业家史编辑部）
　　　　　010-63567683（经济与管理学术编辑部）
　　　　　010-63538621 63567692（发行部）
网　　址：www.edpbook.com.cn
E - m a i l：edpbook@126.com
经　　销：全国新华书店
印　　刷：天津中印联印务有限公司
开　　本：880mm×1230mm　1/32
印　　张：4.75
字　　数：76 千字
版　　次：2022 年 9 月第 1 版
印　　次：2022 年 9 月第 1 次印刷
书　　号：ISBN 978-7-5196-1165-1
定　　价：79.00 元

目录

★ chapter ★

小 序
Simple preamble

吾年已不惑，陋习颇多，时常说话招人厌烦，行事让人憎恨，预定好的计划半途而废，设置好的目标事与愿违。为人处世的道理似乎都已明白，并能口若悬河地教育他人，但是自己往往却背道而驰，不加节制、不善敬畏，导致与社会与家庭不能和谐，工作和生活上不能顺畅。

There is a saying in China that people will not be confused when they are 40 years old, which is my age now. However, I still have a lot of bad habits, for example, some people don't like what I say, they don't want to communicate with me deeply, and I do things that cause them to hate. The plans I set for myself often fall by the wayside, and the goals I set often fail to reach them. I seem to have understood the truth of being a person and doing things, and can educate others with eloquence, but I often do not abide by these principles. I am not good at controlling, not good at awing, they often cause me not to live in harmony with society and family, and not to be smooth and happy in work and life.

所以，人生需要总结提炼，让自己全面地反思，通透地领悟，并形成文字，希望可以提醒自己，至少在迷茫纠结的时候可以从哲学层面自我开解。

Therefore, life needs to be summed up and refined, so that you can comprehensively reflect and understand, and organize them into words. I hope this can remind myself that I can enlighten myself on a philosophical level at least when I am confused and tangled.

吾儿年已十八，步入成人，不希望他如我一般经历太多困扰，早点认识一些朴素道理以及实用的方法。在成长中再去实践、去感悟、去升华。在他未来漫长而繁杂的人生道路上，让这些道理和方法带给他力量，带给他温暖。

在他孤立无助的时候，有一处可以让灵魂歇息的港湾。

My son is 18 years old and an independent adult. I don't want him to experience too many troubles like me, and I hope he can get to know some simple truths and practical methods sooner. And in the process of his growth, he will practice, comprehension, and sublimate. On his long and complicated life road in the future, let these principles and methods bring him strength and warmth. When he was alone and helpless, there was a haven for the soul to rest.

于是，我们共同创作了这本小书，他妈妈也参与了校对，并提出了自己的建议，配上插图，翻译成英文。送亲戚、

送朋友、给读者，就当是我们和大家一次真诚、质朴的交流吧。

So, we co-created this little book, his mother also participated in proofreading, and made her own suggestions, accompanied by illustrations, and translated into English. Sending relatives, friends, and readers should be regarded as a sincere and pure exchange between us and you.

书的原名叫《观世微言》，后与朋友三人在中国深圳波托菲诺小聚，谈及此举，友人说，前人有《弟子规》，这本书可取名《与子书》，很适合天下父母子女阅读借鉴，另外一位朋友当即拍案连连叫好。

The original name of the book was "A Little View on World ". Later, I had a small gathering with three friends in Portofino, Shenzhen, China, and talked about this matter. A friend said that there was a famous book "Student Regulation" in ancient China. This book can be called "A Book for Gentlemen", because it is also very suitable for parents and children all over the world to read and learn from. Another friend immediately applauded it.

聚会是在湖边露天餐厅，当时已是黄昏时刻，天色渐暗，湖中有一小岛，距离岸边很近，岛上树木郁郁葱葱，谈话间，突然岛上数百喜鹊在树林上空大声追逐、鸣叫、嬉戏，甚是热闹，友人笑称："这是百鸟朝凤啊"，遂坚定此书名。

The party was in an open-air restaurant by the lake. It was already dusk, and the sky was gradually darkening. There is a small island in the center of the lake, which is very close to the shore, and the island is lush with trees. While we were talking, hundreds of birds suddenly appeared on the island, chasing, chirping, and frolic over the woods, very lively. Friends laughed and said, "This is the scene of a hundred birds congratulate the phoenix." They are also congratulating the birth of this book! So I think it's a good name for the book.

《与子书》是一本与君子交流的书，一本赠与子女的书，也是世人、朋友给予我自己的一本书。书虽小，道理却很朴素、适用；名虽简，情意却很真切、温暖。

"A Book for Gentlemen" is a book for communicating with gentlemen, a book for children, and a book for myself from the world and my friends. Although the book is small, the principles are simple and applicable; although the name is simple, the affection is very real and warm.

世界
The World

春天来了，春风吹走了寒冷，万物苏醒，一粒种子在土壤里发芽了，破土而出，长出了鲜嫩的叶子。

Spring is here, the spring wind blows away the cold, everything wakes up, a seed germinates in the soil, breaks out of the soil, and grows fresh leaves.

怀胎十月的小张夫妻，终于生下了一对双胞胎姐弟，也是在这个春天里。

The Xiao Zhang couple, who were pregnant for ten months, finally gave birth to a pair of twins, also in this spring.

冬眠的虫子和狗熊也都出来了，太阳也转回来了，大地上开始了春夏秋冬新的一年。

The hibernating bugs and bears have also come

out, the sun has turned back, and the earth has begun a new year of spring, summer, autumn and winter.

在宇宙中，这些都是我们可以看得见的事物，宇宙深处我们看不见的事物是什么样的呢？它们也是在按照自身的规律、演化的轨道，在运行、在转换。它们的表现方式无穷无尽，都在适应着它所处的环境，和其他的物种相互影响、相互作用。

In the universe, these are all things we can see. In the depths of the universe, how do things that we can't see appear? They are also running and transforming according to their own laws and evolutionary tracks. Their expressions are endless, all adapting to their environment, interacting with other species and interacting with each other.

我们看得见的世界，明显可以分为动物和植物两种类型。植物普遍表现为不会说话，不会移动，不会思考。而动物会说话，会移动，会思考。尤其是人，最善于思考。

The visible world can be clearly divided into two

types: animals and plants. Plants generally can not speak, can not move, and can not think. Animals can talk, move, and think. People, in particular, are the best at thinking.

很多人认为人是有灵魂的，人分为肉体和灵魂两个部分。但是这里认为，人和其他的动物相比，只是基因不一样。而且人类的基因更优质，更善于思考，优质的基因造就了思想的千差万别、形形色色的人类。不同的基因造就了人不同的性格，也致使他们拥有不同的命运。

Many people think that human beings have a soul, and that human beings are divided into two parts, the body and the soul. But here it is believed that compared with other animals, humans are only genetically different. And human genes are better and better at thinking, and high-quality genes have created human beings with different thoughts and all kinds of people. Different genes create different personalities of people, and also cause them to have different destinies.

人的学习能力也比其他动物要强很多，通过学习和实践可以改变命运，也可以让自身的基因呈现出最好的一面，显得更加健康、更加聪明。

Human's learning ability is also much stronger than that of other animals. Through learning and practice, we can change our destiny, and we can also make our genes show the best side, which appears healthier and smarter.

我们还发现一棵小草的生老病死，人与动物的生老病死，它们内在规律和道理都是相通的。按照这个推理，宇宙间是万物相连、道理相通的。

We also found that the birth, aging, illness and death of a grass, and the birth, aging, illness and death of humans and animals, their internal laws and principles are interlinked. According to this reasoning, everything in the universe is connected, and the reason is the same.

以上是对世界的观察，但是，我们在这里只关注我们人类的自身，分析一下人应该如何生活和工作？

The above is an observation of the world, but here we only focus on our own human beings and analyze how people should live and work?

人要面对的主要就是健康问题、安全问题、经济问题、思想问题，以及与人交往的方式方法问题，这些问题是否存在一些朴素而简单的真理？答案是肯定的。

The main issues that people have to face are health issues, safety issues, economic issues,

ideological issues, and the ways and means of interacting with people. Are there some simple truths about these issues? The answer is yes.

归根结底，人追求的是幸福和快乐，如何最大程度地满足我们的这个需求呢？这些都是我们这里需要剖析和呈现的。

In the final analysis, what people pursue is happiness, how to meet our needs to the greatest extent? These are all we need to analyze and present here.

生 命

Life

一棵小树

如果没有了水会怎么样？没有了空气会怎么样？没有了土壤会怎么样？没有了阳光会怎么样？

A small tree

What if there is no water? What would happen without air? What happens without soil? What would happen without the sun?

一个人

想一下，口渴找不到水喝的滋味；没有空气几分钟就会窒息而死；没有土壤就没有食物，几天就会饿死；地球如果没有阳光的温暖，就会和宇宙深处一样寒冷，达到零下几百度，地球将是一片荒野，毫无生机。

One person

Think about it, if you are thirsty, you will not find the taste of water; if there is no air, you will suffocate to death in a few minutes; if there is no soil, there will be no food, and you will starve to death in a few days; if the earth does not have the warmth of sunlight, it will be the same as the depths of the universe. When it is cold, reaching hundreds of degrees below zero, the earth will be a wilderness and lifeless.

人和万物一样，都需要一个良好的环境，需要水、空气、土壤和阳光，这是我们生存的基本条件。

Like all things, people need a good environment, water, air, soil and sunlight, which are the basic conditions for our survival.

所以我们最应该注重这些生存的基本因素，喝干净的水，待在空气清新的地方，注意摄取均衡的营养，冬天的时候多晒晒太阳，它会让我们拥有一个健康的身体。

除此之外，那些生命的非必需品，如过量的食物、毒品、烟、酒则会损害我们的身体，扰乱我们的生活。

Therefore, we should pay attention to these basic factors of survival, drink clean water, stay in a place with fresh air, pay attention to ingesting balanced nutrition, and get more sun in winter, it will make us have a healthy body.

In addition, those non-essentials of life, such as excessive food, drugs, tobacco, alcohol will damage our body and disrupt our life.

清淡简朴的生活习惯非常必要，山珍海味、锦衣玉食往往是精神上错误的引导。很多时候它们是为了体现所谓高贵的身份，对身体并没有好处。酒肉再贵，酒池肉林也都是埋葬我们的坟墓；过于奢华的房子也并不适合健康居住；放纵带给我们的快乐总是短暂的，自然恬淡的生活才是最长久和舒适的；千年的参天大树也仅仅需要充足的水分、空气、土壤和阳光。

Light and simple living habits are very necessary, and delicacies from mountains and seas, fine clothes and jade food are often the wrong guidance in spirit. Many times they are to reflect the so-called noble status and are not good for the body. No matter how precious wine and meat are, wine ponds and meat forests are often our graves; too large and luxurious houses are not suitable for healthy living; the happiness that indulgence brings us is always short-lived, and the natural and tranquil life is the longest and most comfortable; thousand-year-old towering sky large trees also only need sufficient water, air, soil and sunlight.

中国古代很多帝王骄奢淫逸，饭来张口、衣来伸手，年纪轻轻就死去。人类的很多疾病都是吃得"太好了"，生活得"太舒服了"，没有适当的劳动和锻炼引起的。大家都会认可这些道理，但是真正重视的人却很少，能约束自己行为的人更是少之又少。

In ancient China, many emperors were arrogant and extravagant. Many human diseases are caused by eating "too good" and living "too comfortable" without proper labor and exercise. Once these truths are said, everyone will agree, but very few people

really pay attention to them, and even fewer people can restrain their behavior.

人在年轻的时候由于身体素质好，往往不能体会到健康的重要性，不注重养生和自律。总是在生病的时候盼望自己好起来，老的时候希望自己是健康的。

When people are young, due to their good physical fitness, they often fail to appreciate the importance of health and do not pay attention to health preservation and self-discipline. Always hope that you will get better when you are sick, and hope that you will be healthy when you are old.

人很容易就能了解健康养生的方法和道理，但是很少人能做到,这可怎么办呢？能够意识到健康养生的重要性，制定出好的生活作息计划，并且坚持直至养成习惯，当然是最好的。如果做不到，那就让一切顺其自然吧。但是，一定需要明白这些道理，在这些道理的引导下，不能全部做到，偶尔做一下也是不错的，潜移默化中，说不定哪一天就会唤起我们的力量，让我们的生活变得更好。

It is easy for people to understand the methods

and principles of health preservation, but few people can do it. What can we do? It is of course the best to be able to realize the importance of health preservation, formulate a good life schedule, and stick to it until a habit is formed. If you can't, just let it all take its course. However, we must understand these principles. Under the guidance of these principles, we cannot do all of them, but it is good to do it occasionally. In subtle ways, maybe one day it will arouse our strength and improve our life.

我们看到的世界是"假的"，因为我们看世界的能力和方法远远不够，大约只有百分之五，百分之九十五的世界我们现在还看不到。

The world we see is "fake", because our ability and method to see the world is far from enough, only about 5%, 95% of the world we can't see yet.

时间是依据太阳与地球的相互运动规律设立的，所以时间本质就是运动。

Time is established according to the law of

mutual motion between the sun and the earth, so the essence of time is motion.

通过录像回放，我们可以复原 10 小时之前地球的运动轨迹。随着科技的发展，也许世界影像、人类活动都可以通过倒放看到过去。同样，如果掌握了正确的原理，也可以快放到未来。因为他们都是按照一定的规律在变化，在流逝。

Through video playback, we can restore the trajectory of the earth 10 hours ago. With the development of science and technology, perhaps the world's images and human activities can be viewed backwards. Likewise, if the correct principles are grasped, it can also be fast-forwarded into the future. Because they are all changing and passing according to certain laws.

未来的经历很多是现在的行动决定的。但是，人类情感是复杂的，又是随机的。思想会改变当下的行动，也就改变了一部分未来。所以，生命在于行动是非常科学的解释，如人类普遍喜欢的旅游探险！因为它会带来不同的生命体验。

Much of the future experience is determined by the actions of the present. However, human emotions are complex and random. Thoughts change actions in the present, and they change a part of the future. Therefore, life lies in action is a very scientific explanation, such as travel adventures that humans generally like! Because it will bring a different life experience.

生命本来就是一场旅行与探索。

Life is a journey and exploration.

金 钱
Money

　　植物物竞天择，低等动物弱肉强食，它们都很难改变自己所处的自然环境，紧紧地依托着水、空气、土壤、阳光这些基本的生命要素。

　　Plants compete by natural selection, and low-level animals are eaten by the strong, and it is difficult for them to change the natural environment in which they live, relying closely on the basic elements of life such as water, air, soil, and sunlight.

　　在丛林中，一棵小树苗想要成为参天大树，根部要努力地向下延伸，获取更多的营养，树干努力地向上生长，获得充足的阳光，它要尽量多地占有资源，在它的周围竞争者难以生存，只常见一些顽强的小花、小草。动物之间，就靠肉体拼杀，强者为王。

In the jungle, if a small sapling wants to become a towering tree, its roots must extend downward to obtain more nutrients, and its trunk must grow upward to obtain sufficient sunlight. It must occupy as many resources as possible. It is difficult for the surrounding competitors to survive, and only some tenacious small flowers and grasses are common. Between animals, they fight with their bodies, and the strong is king.

但是人类就不同，人类的聪明才智不仅可以改变一些自己赖以生存的自然环境，而且还发明了货币，把金钱和物质、资源、地位、权力一一对应起来，让金钱成为工具，来管理影响人类自身，并且形成了一套全面有效的经济规律，使钱多的人可以支配和奴役钱少的人，形成了金字塔式的阶层。

But human beings are different. Human ingenuity can not only change some of the natural environment on which they live, but also invent money, which maps money to material, resources, status, and

power one by one, making money a tool to manage and influence human beings, who have formed a set of comprehensive and effective economic laws, so that those with more money can dominate and enslave those with less money, forming a pyramid-like hierarchy.

著名的雨果小说《悲惨世界》中，描写了这样一个故事：一个纯真简单的花季少女芳汀，在富二代花花公子们的安排下，她和她的姐妹们兴奋地享受着一整天的假期和爱情，沉浸在美好的梦幻中。但这些对于她们的富二代男友们而言，只不过是他们设置的一个好玩而"浪漫"的游戏。抛弃之前被无情地玩弄，留下未婚生子的芳汀从此一步步滑向人生的深渊。为了换得五十法郎为女儿治病，被老板剪去漂亮的头发，拔掉两颗漂亮的门牙。后来失去美貌的她无奈沦为街头最下层的妓女，充满原始的血腥和冷酷。看着这个故事，我是久久不能释怀，感觉非常不适。试想，如果年轻漂亮的女主角芳汀不被金钱所支配奴役，不被社会阶层所压榨，会是那样悲惨的人生吗？

In the famous Hugo novel "Les Miserables",

there is such a story: an innocent girl Fantine, under the arrangement of the rich second-generation sons, she and her sisters are excited to enjoy a whole day of vacation and love. But these are just a fun and "romantic" game they set up for their rich second-generation boyfriends. After the ruthless play, they left with satisfaction, but Fantine became pregnant, and she slipped into the abyss of life step by step. In exchange for fifty francs to treat the illegitimate daughter, Fantine was cheated by the black-hearted boss to cut off her beautiful hair and pulled out two white front teeth. The whole story is full of raw gore and grimness. Looking at this story, I couldn't let go for a long time, and I felt very uncomfortable. Just imagine, if the young and beautiful heroine Fantine was not enslaved by money and squeezed by social class, would she have such a miserable life?

所以，金钱是人类生存和发展的基础，人的第一要务是建立好这个基础，并且要保护好这个基础，否则一切都无从谈起，都是空中楼阁，失去了金钱的保护，人生可能就会堕入悲惨的世界中。

Therefore, money is the foundation of human survival and development. The first priority of human beings is to establish this foundation and protect it. Otherwise, everything will be impossible and it will be a castle in the air. Without the protection of money, life may end into a miserable world.

如何才能有钱，每个人的方式方法都不一样，但是有钱无非两种途径，一是继承，二是赚钱。如何才能赚到钱？方法非常多，但是有没有一个基本的要求？答案是肯定的，我们来分析一下：赚钱的前提就是别人愿意给你钱才行，那么为什么别人愿意给你钱呢？这里有个关键词就是"愿意"，人在什么情况下会愿意做一些事情呢？想想我们自己，别人怎么做才会让自己愿意为他付出金钱呢？

How to get rich, everyone has different ways and methods, but there are only two ways to have money, one is inheritance, and the other is to make money. How can I make money? There are many methods, but is there a basic requirement? The answer is yes, let's analyze it: the premise of making money is that others are willing to give you money, so why are others willing to give you money? A key word here is "willing". Under what circumstances would people be willing to do something? Think about ourselves, how can others make themselves willing to pay for them?

人的思想来自认知，比方说这个人认为你是好人，那么你在他那里就是好人，无论你是流氓还是罪犯。有人喜欢吃萝卜，不喜欢吃辣椒，也有人喜欢吃辣椒，不喜欢吃萝卜，这个就和他的口味和爱好有关，和辣椒萝卜到底哪个更好没有关系。

认为你是好人就愿意和你相处，喜欢吃的食物就愿意去吃，否则，你人再好，别人也不认可你，食物再昂贵、营养价值再高别人也不愿意食用。很多人只站在自己的立场和角度上去判定、要求别人，往往得不到他想要的结果。

Human thinking comes from cognition. For example, if this person thinks you are a good person,

then you are a good person for him, whether you are a rogue or a criminal. Some people like to eat radishes and don't like to eat chili peppers, and some people like to eat chili peppers and don't like to eat radishes. This has to do with their tastes and hobbies, and it has nothing to do with which is better with chili peppers and radishes.

If others think you are a good person, he will be willing to get along with you. Otherwise, no matter how nice you are, others will not recognize you, and he will be willing to eat the food that others like to eat. Otherwise, no matter how expensive and nutritious the food is, others will not be willing to eat it. Many people only judge and ask others from their own standpoint and perspective, but they often don't get the results they want.

中国古代宫廷有太监，诸多朝代都有宦官弄权现象，王侯将相都被他们玩弄于股掌之间，他们甚至可以毁掉一个朝代，不是这些太监们有多大的学问和本领，而是他们

深谙伺候人这门技术，把皇帝伺候得舒舒服服，让皇帝离不开他们，皇帝就愿意给他们权力，愿意骄纵他们，哪怕知晓他们祸国殃民，可能仍是一味庇佑迁就。这使得这些太监金钱无数，权力无边。

There were eunuchs in the ancient court of China. In many dynasties, they had great power. Generals and princes had to submit to them, and they could even destroy a dynasty. Not because these eunuchs have great knowledge and skills, but because they are very good at serving people. They e made the emperor's service comfortable and made the emperor inseparable from them. The emperor was willing to give them power and indulge them. Even if they were a disaster to the country and the people, he might just bless and accommodate them, so that these eunuchs had countless money and boundless power.

让人"愿意"其实就是驭人之术，务必要洞悉和你交往的人的需求，人的需求是多种多样、五花八门的，有人追求梦想，有人需要激情，有人喜欢被赞美，有人需要倾诉，有人需求理解，有人爱慕金钱，有人醉心于权力、地位。

Making people "willing" is actually the art of controlling people. You must understand the needs of the people you are dealing with. People's needs are diverse and varied. Some people pursue their dreams, some people need passion, some people like to be praised, and some people need to pour out, some people need to be understood, some people love money, some people are addicted to power and status.

掌握这个人的需求之后，分析自己的资源，看哪些可以满足他，就给他，现有的条件下无法满足的看能否在未来或者经过努力满足他？满足别人需求的方法可能有千万种，不停地探索，不停地给予，就会变得游刃有余，左右逢源。如果你能顺利做到这一点，就会发现赚钱就会变成一件很简单的事情。

After mastering the needs of this person, analyze your own resources, then see what can satisfy him, and give them to him. Can those that cannot be

satisfied under the existing conditions be satisfied in the future or after efforts? There may be thousands of ways to meet the needs of others. Keep exploring and giving, and you will become more and more comfortable. If you do this successfully, you will find that making money becomes a very simple thing.

诸多文人学者愤青往往不屑于投其所好，认为这是一件低贱的事情，非大丈夫所为，其实大才大德之人应该拥有广阔的胸怀，带领别人踏上梦想之旅，让别人如沐春风，这是一种智慧和能力啊！

Many literati and scholars often disdain to go against their own ideas to cater to other people's hobbies, thinking that doing such a lowly thing is not a man's act. In fact, a person with great talent and great virtue should have a broad mind, lead others to embark on a dream journey, and make others feel like a spring breeze. This is a kind of wisdom and ability!

人生之美，人生之幸福，不一定是一味狭隘地满足自己当前的欲望和已有的认知，换一种方式，带给别人幸福感，

带给别人价值和意义，人生也会如诗如画，会让你得到更多。

The beauty and happiness of life is not necessarily to blindly satisfy one's current desires and existing cognitions. In another way, to bring happiness to others, to bring value and meaning to others, life will be picturesque and give you more.

动辄就讲自己如何如何的人，大多不能富贵；一味强调自己感受的人，大多很少朋友，成为孤家寡人。快意恩仇固然爽，孤芳自赏也很酷，自私自大也是你的自由，但是这带给我们的往往是坎坷和挫折，甚至是性命之灾。

People who talk about how they are at every turn will rarely become wealthy people; those who only emphasize their own feelings will have few friends. Doing things according to your own likes and dislikes often feels very happy, and it often feels cool to put yourself in a high position. It is your freedom to choose to be a selfish and arrogant person, but it often brings us ups and downs and setbacks, even life danger.

为 人
The Right Person

对于喜欢逛街的人来说，琳琅满目的商品和目不暇接的建筑能激发他们的好奇心，产生吸引力，他们经常是兴致勃勃、流连忘返。但是如果让他们站到街道两边的高楼顶上往下看，街道一下子就变得很简单，一目了然，他们估计就没有了原来的兴致，甚至会顿感索然无味。这正是"不识庐山真面目，只缘身在此山中。"很多事情只有置身事外，从更高的维度来看问题，才能看得清楚，才不会被表象左右。

For people who like to go shopping, the dazzling array of goods and dizzying buildings have stimulated their curiosity and attracted them, and they are often enthusiastic and lingering. But if you let them stand on the top of the tall buildings on both sides of the street and look down, the street will suddenly become very simple, and at a glance, it is estimated that they will lose their original interest, and even feel dull. This is precisely because he does not know the true face of Mount Lu, only because he is in this mountain. Many things can only be seen clearly by looking from a higher dimension, and then people will not be swayed by appearances.

从飞机上看，偌大的城市显得很小；从太空中看地球，地球就像是一个蓝色的玩具小皮球；从宇宙的视角来看，地球就相当于一粒尘埃了。那么，我们处在地球表面的人，又是多么的渺小啊，就像我们身体里只能用显微镜才能看见的细菌一样。

From the plane, the huge city looks very small; from space, the earth is like a small blue toy ball; from the perspective of the universe, the earth is equivalent to a speck of dust. Then, how small are we on the surface of the earth, just like the bacteria in our body that can only be seen with a microscope.

对于博大的宇宙，人类如同看不见的细菌，但是，对

于很多人来说，自己可是比宇宙还大，因为那里是一个自己的世界，有爱恨情仇，有喜怒哀乐，有无数想象中的画面，所有的这一切占据他整个的思维和情感，让他沉迷其中，无法自拔。很少有人会这样想：如果从宇宙这个视角来看自己，就像是个微不足道、看不见的细菌。也如人看自己脚下的蚂蚁，没有人会去关心它的喜怒哀乐，甚至极少人会在乎它的生死。

To the vast universe, human beings are like invisible bacteria. However, for many people, they are bigger than the universe, because there is a world of their own, with love, hatred, joys and sorrows, and countless imaginations. The picture, all of which occupied his entire thinking and emotion, made him addicted to it, and unable to extricate himself from transcendence. Few people think that if you look at yourself from the perspective of the universe, you are like a trivial, and invisible germ. Just like a person looking at an ant under his feet, no one cares about its joys and sorrows, and even very few people care about its life and death.

所以，我们为人不可妄自尊大，陷入自我感觉之中。很多时候，自己认为过不去、非常重要的东西，只是你自己一个人的想法而已，并没有人会关心，会当回事。

Therefore, we must not be arrogant as human beings and get caught up in self-awareness. A lot of times, the things that you think are difficult and very important are just your own thoughts, and no one will care about them and take them seriously.

二战时期，英国首相丘吉尔接受英国广播公司 BBC 的邀请做一个直播演讲，半路上他乘坐的专车出了状况。此时恰巧有一辆出租车经过，他赶紧拦下，让司机送他去 BBC 公司。司机却说："我送你过去要绕道，会耽误我听偶像丘吉尔的演讲。"丘吉尔一听，心想自己在别人心里原来这么重要，于是掏出五英镑递给司机，让司机载他过去。司机立即收下钱并说："去他的丘吉尔吧，您上车，我这就载您过去。"这件事让丘吉尔感触颇深：别太把自己当回事，你可能连五英镑都不值。

During World War II, British Prime Minister

Winston Churchill accepted the invitation of the BBC to give a live speech, and the special car he was riding on the way broke down. At this time, a taxi happened to pass by, and he quickly stopped him and asked the driver to take him to the BBC company. But the driver said, "I have to take a detour to take you there, which will delay my listening to my idol Churchill's speech." When Churchill heard it, he thought that he was so important in others' hearts, so he took out five pounds and handed it to the driver to let the driver take him there. The driver immediately took the money and said, "Go to his Churchill, you get in the car, and I'll take you there." This incident made Churchill feel deeply: don't take yourself too seriously, you might not even be worth five pounds.

德国有句谚语："只有在人群中间，才能认识自己。"这个世界上每个人有每个人的烦恼，各人有各人的生活，千万别以为所有人都会把精力放在你身上。做人，无论拥有多少东西，处于何种地位，一定要记住，千万不要高估自己的重要性。

There is a German proverb: "Only in the middle of the crowd can you know yourself." In this world, everyone has their own troubles and their own lives. Don't think that everyone will put their energy on you. Be a person, no matter how many things you have or what status you are in, you must remember that you should never overestimate your importance.

人是渺小的，但是人的世界可以是无穷大的，这是因为人和其他植物动物不同，人拥有发达的思想。人的思想分为哪些方面呢？人的外在和表现，长得漂不漂亮，有没有气质，一望便知。但是思想是看不见的，只能靠推理。所以掌握人的思想的主要构成是非常重要的，这是了解一个人的必修课。

Humans are small, but the world of human beings can be infinite. This is because human beings are different from other plants and animals who have developed thoughts. What are the aspects of human thought? The appearance and performance of a person, whether they are beautiful or not, and whether they have temperament, can be known at a glance. But thought is invisible and can only rely on reasoning. Therefore, it is very important to grasp the main components of the human mind, which is a required course for understanding a person.

人的思想主要来源于环境、学习、经历等等，其中最基础、最核心的就是欲望，物质和精神上的欲望，其他都是欲望的表现形式。

People's thoughts mainly come from the environment, learning, experience, etc. The most basic and core of them are desires, material and spiritual desires, and the rest are the manifestations of desires.

物质的欲望无非就是金钱和物品，精神上的欲望实际上就是心理满足。做人，做别人眼里的好人，就需要有满足别人欲望的能力。如果你还没有能力满足别人的欲望该怎么办呢？那就让他相信你能满足他的欲望。如果别人相

信了你，就和真正满足他有同样的效果。这也可以得到别人的认可，并且可以用来左右别人的行动和思想。"望梅止渴"的故事大家都知道吧？

Material desires are nothing more than money and goods, and spiritual desires are actually psychological satisfaction. To be a person, to be a good person in the eyes of others, is to have the ability to satisfy the desires of others. What should you do if you don't have the ability to satisfy other people's desires? Then convince him that you can satisfy his desires. If someone trusts you, it has the same effect as truly satisfying him. It can also be recognized by others, and can be used to influence the actions and thoughts of others. Everyone knows the story of "Quench Your Thirst by looking at plums"?

总之一句话，要么真的满足别人的欲望，要么让别人坚信你可以满足他的欲望，这是为人最核心的思想。如果你想得到你想要的，这个是必须要做到的。有两种人，一

种人是通过满足别人的需求而得到自己想要的；另外一种人是不停地千方百计地索取，想得到自己想要的。你想成为哪种人呢？

In a word, either really satisfy other people's desires, or make others believe that you can satisfy their desires. This is the core idea of being a human being. If you want to get what you want, this must be done. There are two kinds of people. One kind of people gets what they want by meeting the needs of others; the other kind of people keeps trying to get what they want. What kind of person do you want to be?

为人另外一种素质也是非常重要的，那就是节制。关于节制的故事很多，这里我讲一个自己的真实经历。一段时间我迷上了香辣蟹，开始吃的时候很开心，幸福感满满，就一连吃了半个月，天天去吃，导致我现在一闻到香辣蟹的味道就感觉不舒服。香辣蟹的味道没有变，可是由于我的不节制，失掉了香辣蟹带给我的快乐和幸福感。

Another quality of being a person is also very

important, that is moderation. There are many stories about moderation. Here I will tell you a real experience. I fell in love with spicy crab for a while. When I started to eat it, I was very happy and full of happiness, I ate it for half a month in a row, and went to eat it every day. As a result, I now feel uncomfortable when I smell the spicy crab. The taste of the spicy crab has not changed, but because of my intemperance, I have lost the joy and happiness that the spicy crab brought me.

很多人认为想吃就吃，想睡就睡，或者想干什么就干什么这才是自由，可实际上这些只是自己的本能而已，并非自由。真正的自由，不是你想做什么，就去做什么，而是你不想做什么，就不用做什么！

Many people think that eating when they want, sleeping when they want, or doing whatever they want is freedom, but in fact these are just their own instincts, not freedom. The real freedom is not what you want to do, you can do it, but what you don't want to do, you don't need to do it!

　　所有最好的，不过是刚刚好。节制，是一种智慧，是一种自由，更是一种幸福。当你懂得节制时，人生的智慧、生命的自由、生活的幸福定会如约而至。

　　All the best, is just right. Moderation is a kind of wisdom, a kind of freedom, and a kind of happiness. When you know self-control, the wisdom of life, the freedom of life, and the happiness of life will come as promised.

处 世
Get Along With Others

我们认识了生命健康的本质，赚钱的重要性，为人的基本要领，但是如何运用，就是处世的能力了。

We know the essence of life and health, the importance of making money and the basic essentials of being a human being, but how to use it is the ability to live in the world.

很多道理明明都知道了，就是做不到，这是因为人是感情动物，也就是喜欢感情用事。另外，许多外在因素也在影响你的行为，比如，被别人打骂你会很生气，丧失理智；喝醉了酒的时候爱胡说八道，不计后果。我们经常相信自己看到的事情和听到的言论，当这些对自己很不利的时候，我们会立即做出过激的应对措施，但是，这些事情也许并不是和我们看到和听到的那样，我们被假象蒙蔽了。

Many truths are clearly known, but they cannot be done. This is because people are emotional animals, that is, they like to be emotional. In addition, many external factors are also affecting your behavior, such as being beaten and scolded by others will make you angry and lose your sense; when you are drunk, you love to talk nonsense without reckoning with the consequences. We often believe what we see and hear when these remarks are unfavorable to us, and we will immediately take drastic measures, but these things may not be what we see and hear, and we are deceived by illusions.

每个人往往都或多或少已经养成了一些不良的习惯，这些是很难改过来的。人无完人，指的就是这个意思。那有没有办法尽量规避这些问题呢？

Everyone often has more or less developed some bad habits, which are difficult to change. No one is perfect, that's what it means. Is there any way to avoid these problems as much as possible?

推荐的办法有一个，那就是三思而后行，扬长不避短。

An effective method is recommended, that is, when encountering things, think in multiple directions first, and then take action. Promote our strengths and don't dwell too much on our weaknesses.

一定要养成遇到事情多思考的习惯，特别是重大事情，要多想想这样决策会给你带来哪些麻烦和损伤。千万不要图一时之快，只想着好事，甚至自己欺骗自己。

You must develop the habit of thinking more when you encounter things, especially important things. Think more about what troubles and damages such a decision will bring to you. Don't try to be quick, just think about good things, or even deceive yourself.

因为人都是喜欢好事情的，思维的惯性也是凡事首先总是往好处想，期望自己得到什么而潜意识地会忽略风险，所以就需要养成自我提醒的习惯，避免不经意掉进别人设置好的陷阱中。

这里扬长不避短的意思是不要过于纠结自己的短处，而是发扬自己的长处。

Because people like good things, the inertia of thinking is always to think about the good in everything first, expecting something from oneself, and subconsciously ignoring risks. Therefore, you need to develop the habit of reminding yourself to avoid falling into the trap set by others inadvertently.

The idea here is to focus not so much on your weaknesses but on your strengths.

我们人类的历史中英雄伟人辈出，拿破仑、牛顿、爱因斯坦、秦始皇、毛泽东，而且每个时代也都有自己耀眼的明星，然而仔细探索他们的生活和作为，就会发现，他们之中的一些人在一些事情上表现得并不好，有些是那么的不堪，甚至挑战你的三观，因为故事太多，一查便知，这里就不一一列举了。但是，这些都无法掩盖他们的光芒，无法阻挡他们的成就，因为他们的长处太强大，而且发挥得很好。

There are many heroes and great men in our

human history, such as Napoleon, Newton, Einstein, Qin Shihuang, Mao Zedong. Each era also has its own dazzling star. However, if you look closely at their lives and actions, you will find that they are not very good at some things, and some are even very bad. Their mistakes and bad things are all recorded and easy to find in history, so I won't list them all here. However, none of these can cover up their brilliance and can't stop their achievements. Because their strengths are too powerful and play well.

地球上海洋的面积最大，蔚蓝壮阔，人们喜欢用海纳百川来形容一个人的胸怀，意思是一个人的胸怀应该像大海一样宽广。大海可以接纳包容千万条不同的河流，虽然那些河流都不相同，水质也都不一样，大海一直在那里呈现着自己独特的蔚蓝壮阔，并不会因为其他河流而改变大海的模样。大海这样的自然景观和现象表明，我们在生活和工作中包容是非常重要的，要想自己强大，就需要吐故纳新，胸如大海。

The ocean has the largest area on earth and is

blue and magnificent. People like to use the sea to describe a person's mind, which means that a person's mind should be as broad as the sea. The sea can accommodate thousands of different rivers. Although those rivers are different and the water quality is different, the sea has always presented its own unique blue and magnificent, and it will not change the appearance of the sea because of other rivers. Natural landscapes and phenomena such as the sea show that tolerance is very important in our life and work. If we want to be strong, we need to open our minds and embrace the new, like the sea.

　　人情世故就像一个万花筒，人上一百形形色色，每个民族有每个民族的文化和风俗习惯，每个人有每个人的性格，有每个人的好恶，有每个人的优点和缺点。人情世故在人类身上体现得变幻莫测，要想全部看得明白，做得妥当，几乎是不可能的。它是一门没有定式繁杂的学问，只能要我们去体察、尊重别人的想法和诉求，不要排斥歧视，不要只注重自己的好恶。

Human emotions and habits are like a kaleidoscope, and if there are a hundred people, they are all different. Every nation has its own culture and customs. Different people have different personalities, likes and dislikes, advantages and disadvantages. Human emotions and habits are unpredictable in human beings, and it is almost impossible to understand them all and do them properly. It is not a fixed pattern, but also a very complicated knowledge. We can only be asked to observe and respect the thoughts and demands of others, not to reject discrimination, and not to focus only on our own likes and dislikes.

虽然说一个人很难在人情世故中有完美表现，但是学习能力是一定不可缺少的。一个人的认知是很有限的，从生到死，都是一个不断学习的过程。每天都会知道一些以前不知道的东西，特别是遇到强大的人，可以让我们的学习更快捷。人一旦丧失了学习和思考能力，就意味着大概率会被时代淘汰，因而失去很多新兴的机会。

Although it is difficult for a person to have a

perfect performance in the world, but the ability to learn must be indispensable. A person's cognition is very limited. From birth to death, it is a continuous learning process. Knowing something we didn't know before, especially meeting powerful people, can make our learning faster. Once a person loses the ability to learn and think, it means that he is likely to be eliminated by the times, and therefore lose many emerging opportunities.

古语讲：三人行必有我师焉，活到老学到老，朝闻道夕可死。摒弃自以为是，撕开封闭狭隘的外衣，破茧成蝶，飞舞在鲜花丛中，方可仗剑江湖、风光无限。

There are an old Chinese sayings that go like these: When three people are together, there must be one person who can be my teacher. Live and learn. A man who knows the truth in the morning should have no regrets even if he dies in the evening. In a lifetime, people need to have the requirements and ability to learn, get rid of self-righteousness, and open up

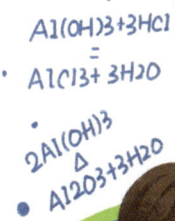

their hearts. If you can do this, you can turn from an ugly cocoon into a beautiful butterfly, flying freely in the flowers, like a top swordsman roaming the rivers and lakes, and the scenery is infinite.

爱因斯坦临终前在给他女儿的信中说，宇宙中最伟大的力量就是爱。其实自然界中的一切美好都来自风调雨顺，来源于上苍爱的施舍。没有上苍的眷爱，我们身边的物种都不会存在。

In his dying letter to his daughter, Einstein said that the greatest force in the universe is love. In fact, all the beauty in nature comes from good weather and from the charity of God's love. Without the grace of God, the species around us would not exist.

中国古代有孟姜女哭长城的传说，孟姜女对丈夫的爱感天动地，甚至哭倒了坚固的长城。现代美国波士顿22岁年轻女子瑞秋将一辆重达2.5吨的越野车抬起，救出被压在下面的父亲，她对父亲的爱让她爆发出超人的力量。人拥有了爱，就会迸发出强大的力量。自古因爱而留下的千古绝唱、惊天动地的人和事数不胜数。

In ancient China, there is a legend of Lady Meng Jiang crying on the Great Wall. Lady Meng Jiang's love for her husband was so moving that she even cried down the strong Great Wall. Rachel, a 22-year-old young woman in modern Boston, lifted a 2.5-ton off-road vehicle to rescue her father who was crushed below. Her love for her father made her burst into superhuman strength. When people have love, they will burst out a powerful force, and there are countless people and events that have been left behind by love since ancient times.

很多人本身属于弱势群体，他们可能会有一个疑问，认为自己本就应该被别人关爱、怜悯，哪还有能力去爱别人？

Many people belong to the disadvantaged group, and they may have a question. They think that they should be cared for and sympathized by others. How can they still have the ability to love others?

回答这个问题可以从两个方面来分析，一是你自己心里需要足够慈悲和强大，不要只站在自己的角度去思考这个问题，而是站在社会需求和规律来选择。二是恐怕你确实需要有足够的物质基础，才符合你施爱的资格，那就去努力赚钱吧。

The answer to this question can be analyzed from two aspects. First, you need to be compassionate and strong in your own heart. You should not only think about this issue from your own perspective, but choose based on social needs and laws. The second is that you really need to have enough material foundation to be eligible for your love. Please start working hard to make money.

世间的矛盾和仇恨哪一个最终不是因为爱才会真正平息，化作无痕？！一切为了爱，生命才能焕发光彩，才可以拥有源源不断的力量。

Which of the contradictions and hatred in the world will not be truly subsided because of love in the end, and will become invisible? ! All for love, then life can be radiant and have a steady stream of power.

勇 敢
Brave

有一个叫丁丁的小山羊，体格强壮，但很胆小。一次比赛中，丁丁连一个狭窄的山谷都不敢跳，妈妈很为丁丁的胆小而担心。有一次，丁丁在大树下等妈妈，一只老虎向它扑了过来，丁丁情急之中慌忙逃跑，它跳过了一个又一个山谷。在丁丁跑到最难跳的山谷时，一下就跳了过去。丁丁妈妈被眼前的情形惊呆了，回家夸奖丁丁真的是太勇敢了。从那以后，丁丁再也不害怕跳山谷了，并且成了草原上的跳远冠军。

There was a little goat named Tintin, who was strong but timid. During a competition, Tintin didn't even dare to jump over a narrow valley, and his mother was very worried about Tintin's cowardice. Once, when Tintin was waiting for his mother under

a big tree, a tiger pounced on him. Tintin fled in a hurry, jumping over one valley after another. When Tintin ran to the most difficult valley to jump, he jumped over. Tintin's mother was stunned by the situation in front of her. She went home and praised Tintin for being really brave. Since then, Tintin was no longer afraid of jumping over the valley, and became the long jump champion on the grassland.

这个故事告诉我们，人在逆境中，只要能鼓起勇气，不怕失败，勇敢面对困难，往往会有意想不到的收获。

This story tells us that in the face of adversity, as long as people can summon the courage, not be afraid of failure, and face difficulties bravely, they will often have unexpected results.

怕怕是一只可爱的小猴子，为什么叫"怕怕"呢？因为他的胆子特别小，不论做什么事情都要妈妈陪在身边，见了人也不爱说话。

Fear is a cute little monkey, why is he called Fear? Because he is very timid, no matter what he does, his mother must be by his side, and he does not like to talk when he meets people.

一天，怕怕的妈妈摔伤了腿，怎么也动不了，怕怕吓得"哇哇"直哭，妈妈让怕怕去请医生松鼠爷爷，但是怕怕自己不敢去。于是妈妈就教给怕怕一个小方法，对怕怕说："好孩子，你害怕的时候就大声说'我是最勇敢的小猴子，我不怕！'这样你就不害怕了。"

One day, Fear's mother broke her leg and couldn't move at all. Fear was so scared that he cried loudly. Fear's mother told Fear to look for Dr. Grandpa Squirrel, but Fear didn't dare to go alone. So Fear's mother taught Fear a little trick, and said to Fear, "Good boy, when you are afraid, say loudly, ' I am the bravest little monkey, I am not afraid! ' That way you won't be afraid."

看着妈妈难受的样子，怕怕只好硬着头皮走出了家门。松鼠爷爷的诊所其实就在怕怕家旁边的大树上，怕怕走着，感觉到自己的心"砰砰"地跳得特别快。来到大树下，树可真高啊！怕怕鼓起勇气，开始爬树。爬着爬着，忽然，

怕怕看见一条毛毛虫。怕怕平时最害怕毛毛虫了，怕怕停了下来，吓得一动也不敢动了。

Seeing Fear's mother's distressed appearance, Fear had to bite the bullet and walked out of the house. Grandpa Squirrel's clinic is actually on the big tree next to the house, and as Fear walks, Fear can feel his heart beating very fast. Fear comes to the big tree, and the tree is really tall! Fear mustered up his courage and began to climb the tree. Crawling and crawling, suddenly, Fear saw a caterpillar. Fear was most afraid of caterpillars, he was afraid that he stopped. Fear didn't dare to move at all.

可是一想起妈妈难受的样子，怕怕暗暗地对自己说："我一定要找到松鼠爷爷，给妈妈看腿！"

But when Fear thought of his mother's uncomfortable appearance, Fear secretly said to himself, "I must find Grandpa Squirrel and treat my mother's legs!"

怕怕这时忽然想起妈妈的话，于是怕怕对自己说："我是最勇敢的小猴子，我不怕！"

At this moment, Fear suddenly remembered what his mother said, so Fear said to himself, "I am the bravest little monkey, I am not afraid!"

可是声音太小，说完还是有些害怕，他又大声说："我是最勇敢的小猴子，我不怕！"然后他慢慢地从毛毛虫旁边爬了上去，一步、两步、三步、四步……怕怕忽然觉得毛毛虫也没有那么可怕了。

But the voice was too low, and he was still a little scared after speaking, then he said loudly, "I am the bravest little monkey, I am not afraid!" Then he slowly climbed up from the caterpillar, one step, two steps, three steps, four steps...Fear suddenly feels that caterpillars are not so scary anymore.

到了树顶，怕怕喘了一口大气，松鼠爷爷听明白了事情的经过，吃惊地看着怕怕说："怕怕，你是自己来的？真是个好孩子！"

When he reached the top of the tree, Fear took a breath, Grandpa Squirrel understood what happened, looked at him in surprise and said, " Fear,you came by yourself? What a good boy!"

在松鼠爷爷精心的医治下，妈妈的腿好得很快。妈妈见人就说："多亏了我的怕怕，要不我的腿还不知道会怎样呢！谁说我们怕怕胆小，其实我的怕怕最勇敢了！"

Under the careful treatment of Grandpa Squirrel, Fear's mother's leg improved very quickly. Seeing people, Fear's mother said, "Thanks to my Fear, otherwise I don't know what would happen to my leg! Who said my Fear were timid, my Fear is the bravest!"

勇敢不是与生俱来的，也需要**锻炼**。在生活中，处处都有锻炼的机会，比如战胜自我。要想战胜自己心中的一些阴影和曾经逃避了的困难，需要坚定的信念和极大的勇气。一旦开始成功地战胜了自我，就可能成为一个真正勇敢的人。

Courage is not innate, it takes practice. In life, there are opportunities for exercise everywhere, such as conquering oneself. It takes firm belief and great courage to overcome some of the shadows in

your heart and the difficulties you have escaped. It is possible to become a truly brave person once you begin to successfully overcome your ego.

有一个寓言，说的是一位老酋长临终对他部落的年轻人说："你们去远行吧，闯荡你们的一生，我送给你们两个信封，第一个信封在你们经历困难的时候可以打开它，另外一个信封等你们在外历练，叶落归根回到部落时再打开它。"

There is a fable about an old chief dying and saying to the young people of his tribe, "You go out into the open world, and I give you two envelopes. When you are going through hard times, you can open the first one. When you return to the tribe after you have roamed the world, open another."

部落的年轻人带着老酋长给他们的信，当遭遇磨难准备退缩的时候，他们打开第一个信封，信封里面有一个小纸条，上面只有三个字："不要怕。"

The young people of the tribe took the letter from the old chief. When they were suffering and were about to back down, they remembered the old chief's words and opened the first envelope. Inside the envelope was a small note with only three words on it: " Don't be afraid."

等他们都人过中年，他们经历过太多的机遇和坎坷，或者是风霜，或者是荣耀，回到部落打开第二个信封，他们看到的是另外三个字："不后悔。"

After reaching middle age, the people of the tribe have experienced too many opportunities and ups and downs, or a lot of wind and frost, or a lot of glory. After returning to the tribe, they opened the second envelope, and all they saw were three other words: "Hava no regrets."

人的一生就是一个过程，并不存在所谓的成功，在这个过程中如何演绎，很多时候取决于自己的勇气，它会让命运尽量掌握在自己的手中。

A person's life is a process, and there is no such thing as success. How to interpret this process often depends on one's own courage. It will let the fate be in one's own hands as much as possible.

面对敌人，面对困难，狭路相逢勇者胜。勇敢可以带给我们力量，勇敢可以带给我们耀眼的光环。

In the face of the enemy, in the face of difficulties, the brave who meet in a narrow way wins. Bravery can bring us strength, and bravery can bring us a dazzling halo.

歌德说过，"你若失去了财产，你只失去了一点；你若失去了荣誉，你就丢掉了许多；你若失去了勇敢，你就丢掉了一切。"

Goethe said, " If you lose wealth, you lose only a little; if you lose honor, you lose a lot; if you lose courage, you lose everything. "

Don't be afraid

Have no regets

面 对
Don't Dodge

相信大家都读过小马过河的寓言故事，这里就让我们重温一下吧。

I believe that everyone has read the fable of the pony crossing the river, so let us revisit it here.

有一天，小马帮老马妈妈驮着半袋麦子准备到磨坊，但被一条小河挡住了去路，河边吃草的老牛说："水很浅，刚没过小腿，能蹚过去。"树上的松鼠却认真地说："水很深，昨天我的一个伙伴就是掉进这条河里淹死的！"

One day, the pony helped the old mama with half a bag of wheat to go to the mill, but was blocked by a small river. The old cow, who was grazing by the river, said, "The water is so shallow that it can just submerge the calf, and you can wade through." The squirrel on the tree said seriously, "The water is very deep. Yesterday one of my buddies fell into this river and drowned!"

小马不知道该听谁的话，就跑回去问妈妈，妈妈告诉他说："孩子，不要光听别人说，自己不动脑筋，不去试试，是不行的。河水是深是浅，你去试一试就会明白了。"

The pony didn't know who to listen to, so he ran back and asked his mother, who told him, "Son, don't just listen to what others say, don't think about it yourself, don't try it, it won't work. Whether the river is deep or shallow, you try it and you'll understand."

小马跑到河边，刚刚抬起前蹄，松鼠就大叫起来："这里水很深，你不要命啦！"小马说："让我试试吧。"小马下了河，小心地蹚了过去。原来，河水既不像老牛说的那样浅，也不像松鼠说的那样深。

The pony ran to the river, and as soon as he lifted his front hooves, the squirrel shouted, "The water is very deep here, you are going to die!" The pony said,

"Let me try." The pony went down the river, carefully wandering over. It turned out that the river was neither as shallow as the old cow said, nor as deep as the squirrel said.

很多事情只有自己去实践，去体会总结，才会了解事情的真相。往往你的所见所闻，你现有的认知，都不一定是对的。不是不听别人的建议，而是不可一味地人云亦云。

Many things can only be understood by practicing and summarizing by yourself. Often what you see and hear, and your existing cognition, are not necessarily correct. It's not that you don't listen to other people's advice, it's that you can't just follow what others said.

躲避是人的天性，因为人们会以为它可以脱离危险，让自己获得安宁，但是躲避会让我们永远找不到正确的答案，让我们永远不能迈过坎坷，迎接阳光，走向未来。

It is human nature to avoid, because people think that it can get out of danger and let themselves find peace, but avoidance will make us never find the right answer, so that we will never be able to go through the bumps, meet the sun, and go to the future.

我曾经在电视节目上看到一个很偏激的故事，一对情侣，感情一直非常好，已经到了谈婚论嫁的地步，但是女孩遭到闺蜜的嫉恨。一天，女孩的闺蜜装作无意透露给男孩一个消息：女孩还有一个男友，现在就在和他约会！

I once saw a very extreme story on a television program. A couple's relationship has always been very good, and it has reached the point of talking about marriage, but the girl is jealous of her girlfriend. One day, the girl's best friend pretended to inadvertently reveal to the boy that the girl has a boyfriend and is now dating him!

男孩赶过去一看，女孩子确实正和另外一个男孩亲密地走在一起。男孩顿时如五雷轰顶，想到自己纯真的感情就这样被玩弄，愤而离去。而这个女孩当时已经怀了男孩的孩子，那天约会的也只是一个普通朋友，她正准备第二天告诉男孩自己怀孕的消息。当女孩第二天找到男孩的时候，男孩又在女孩闺蜜的鼓动下故意和她做一些亲密的动作，刺伤报复女孩，并从此不再理会女孩。

The boy rushed over to see that the girl was indeed walking intimately with another boy. The boy suddenly felt like a thunderclap, thinking that his pure feelings were being played with like this. He left in anger. The girl was already pregnant with the boy's child at that time, and the date was just an ordinary friend. She was about to tell the boy that she was pregnant the next day. When the girl found the boy the next day, the boy deliberately made some intimate actions with the girl's best friend under the instigation of the girl's best friend, to stab the girl in revenge, and he decided to ignore the girl from now on.

女孩子伤心极了，再也不愿意主动去找男孩，自己生下小孩，过着几十年单亲家庭的日子。从此女孩对男孩只有刻骨的怨恨，男孩每每想起自己的初恋，亦是耿耿于怀。

The girl was very sad, and she no longer wanted to take the initiative to find the boy. The girl gave birth to her child by herself, and lived as a single-

parent family for decades. Since then, the girl has only a deep resentment towards the boy, and the boy feels very uncomfortable whenever he thinks of his first love.

机缘巧合下，这对情侣终于知道了事情的真相，了解到这是一个天大的误会的时候，人生大半已经过去，他们已经是两鬓斑白的老人了。

By chance, the couple finally knew the truth of the matter, and when they realized that this was a big misunderstanding, most of their lives had passed, and they were already old men with gray temples.

类似这样的事情在现实生活中其实很多，但凡一方能够积极面对，及时地去沟通交流，都会避免悲剧的发生。有多少人是因为一个误解而长时间无法释怀？又有多少事情是因为一次错误的判断，事后没有弥补和解释而导致误会进一步加深？相信绝大多数人都会有类似的经历吧？

There are actually many things like this in real life, but as long as one can actively face it and communicate in a timely manner, the tragedy will be avoided. How many people are unable to let go for a long time because of a misunderstanding? How many things were misunderstood because of a wrong judgment, and the misunderstanding was further deepened without making up and explaining afterwards? I believe most people will have a similar experience, right?

我们往往认为自己是对的，对得起自己的良知，而不屑去和别人沟通，或者是不愿意放低自己去试图理解别人，这都是造成我们生活困惑的最大因素。别人对你产生的误解，只能靠你自己去积极化解，期待别人改变或者置之不理，大多时候会造成你不愿意看到的结果。

We often think that we are right and worthy of our conscience, and we are disdainful to communicate with others, or we are unwilling to lower ourselves to try to understand others. These are the biggest factors that cause confusion in our lives. Misunderstandings that others have about you can only be actively resolved by yourself. If you always

expect others to change or ignore it, most of the time it will cause results you don't want to see.

艾森豪威尔是美国第 34 任总统，他年轻时经常和家人一起玩纸牌游戏。他的运气特别不好，每次抓到的都是很差的牌。开始时，他只是有些抱怨，后来，他实在是忍无可忍，便发起了少爷脾气。

Eisenhower, the 34th president of the United States, used to play card games with his family when he was young. He's been particularly unlucky, and he's drawn bad hands every time. At the beginning, he just complained a little, but later, he couldn't bear it anymore, so he got angry.

一旁的母亲看不下去了，正色道："既然要打牌，你就必须用手中的牌打下去，不管牌是好是坏。好运气是不可能都让你碰上的！"艾森豪威尔听不进去，依然忿忿不平。母亲于是又说："人生就和这打牌一样，发牌的是上帝。不管你名下的牌是好是坏，你都必须拿着，你都必须面对。你能做的，就是让浮躁的心情平静下来，然后认真对待，把自己的牌打好，力争达到最好的效果。这样打牌，这样对待人生才有意义！"

The mother on the side couldn't stand it anymore, and said sternly, "Since you want to play cards, you must play the cards in your hands, no matter whether the cards are good or bad. You can't come across all good luck!" Eisenhower couldn't hear it, still resentful. The mother then said, "Life is like playing cards, and it is God who deals the cards. No matter whether the cards in your name are good or bad, you must hold them, and you must face them. What you can do is to let the impetuous calm down your mood, take it seriously, play your cards well, and strive to achieve the best results. Playing cards like this and treating life like this will make sense!"

艾森豪威尔此后一直牢记母亲的话，并激励自己去积极进取。就这样，他一步一个脚印地向前迈进，成为中校、盟军统帅，最后登上了美国总统之位。上帝发的牌总是有好有坏，一味埋怨是没有半点用处的，也无法改变现状。

印度前总统尼赫鲁也曾经说过这样一句话："生活就像是

玩扑克，发到手的牌是定了的，但你的打法却取决于自己的意志。"

Eisenhower has since kept his mother's words in mind and inspired himself to be proactive. In this way, he moved forward step by step, becoming a lieutenant colonel, commander-in-chief of the Allied Forces, and finally ascended to the position of President of the United States. There are always good and bad cards dealt by God. Blindly complaining is useless and cannot change the status quo. Former Indian President Nehru also once said this, "Life is like playing poker. The cards dealt are fixed, but the way you play depends on your own will."

这些故事告诉我们，个人所处的环境靠个人也许无力改变，但如何适应环境则是自己完全可以选择的。人的一生难免会碰上许多问题，遇到不少挫折。在面对问题和挫折时，怨天尤人解决不了任何问题。积极调整好自己的情绪，勇敢地迎接人生的挑战，并尽最大的努力去做好每一件事，这才是最佳的选择！

These stories tell us that the environment the individual lives in may not be able to be changed by the individual, but how to adapt to the environment is completely optional. In life, people will inevitably encounter many problems and setbacks. When faced with problems and setbacks, blaming others cannot solve any problems. Actively adjust your emotions, bravely meet the challenges of life, and do your best to do everything well. This is the best choice!

放 下
Drop Them

有位满怀怨恨的妇人向高僧诉说着过去种种的不平，"我如此难过，是因为那个人实在太过分了……"她激动地说。

A woman who was full of resentment told the monk about all kinds of injustices in the past, "I am so sad because that person is too much..." She said excitedly.

"嗯！你的境遇的确悲惨！"高僧说，"但是会让你如此难过的还是你自己呀！"

"Well! Your situation is indeed miserable!" said the eminent monk, "but it is you who will make you so sad!"

"怎么会是我呢？明明是他的错！"

"How could it be me? It's obviously his fault!"

"你的痛苦难道不是你自己的想法造成的吗？"高僧说，"想一想，那个人和那些事都已经过去，你现在的痛苦又从何而来？还不是因为你自己紧抓着过去不放，不是吗？对方也许只伤害过你一次，你却在心中一而再，再而三地反复想着，自己又伤害自己千百次。想想看，他都已经伤害你了，难道你还要对他念念不忘吗？

"Isn't your pain caused by your own thoughts?" the high monk said, "Think about it, that person and those things have already passed, where does your current pain come from? It's because you are clinging to the past. You can't let it go. The other person has only hurt you once, but you think over and over again in your heart, and you hurt yourself thousands of times. Think about it, he has already hurt you, don't you still want to forget him?

放下痛苦，和自己和解，怀揣着一颗平淡从容的心享受生活。关键是我们能否悟出这个道理，愿不愿意去尝试。

Put down the pain, reconcile with yourself,

and enjoy life with a calm and calm heart. The key is whether we can realize this truth and whether we are willing to try it.

人们几乎避免不了会被别人有意或者无意地伤害到，我们选择应对的方式无非就是报复、记恨或者饶恕。

It is almost inevitable that people will be hurt, intentionally or unintentionally, by others, and the way we choose to deal with is nothing more than revenge, resentment, or forgiveness.

如果我们选择报复，肯定会增加新的仇恨。当别人机会到来的时候，也可以选择继续报复我们，这就是我们常说的"冤冤相报何时了"。当然合法合理地保护自己，扬善除恶这些都是应该倡导的。

If we choose to retaliate, new hatreds will certainly be added. When other people have the opportunity, they can choose to continue to take revenge on us, which is trapped in a terrible cycle. Of course, protecting ourselves legally and reasonably, advocating goodness and eradicating evil should all be advocated.

如果我们选择记恨，肯定会影响我们快乐的心情，破坏我们幸福的生活。

If we choose to hold grudges, it will definitely affect our happy mood and destroy our happy life.

如果我们选择饶恕和放下，对我们的伤害也就就此止步了。我们特别不应该计较无心的伤害和合理合法竞争导致的损害。放下它们，就可以不让自己生活在伤害的阴影之中。

If we choose to forgive and let go, the damage to us stops there. In particular, we should not care about unintentional harm and harm caused by reasonable and legitimate competition. By letting go of them, you can keep yourself from living in the shadow of harm.

除了伤害很难让我们释怀之外，人生也有很多遗憾也会让我们不容易释怀，比方说做错了一件事情，经常会让自己追悔莫及，几天、几个月甚至几年都生活在懊悔的阴影里面。

这其实就是完美主义，人世间任何事情想要十全十美几乎是不可能的！何况事物是发展的，现在完美的东西，不代表在未来也是完美的，甚至当初认为是完美的，在未来回头再看，可能还是错误的。

In addition to the hurt that is difficult to let us relieve, there are also many regrets in life that will also make it difficult for us to let go. For example, if we do something wrong, we often make ourselves regret it, and live for a few days, months or even years in the shadow of regret.

This is actually perfectionism. It is almost impossible to be perfect in anything in this world! What's more, things are developing. What is perfect now does not mean that it will be perfect in the future. Even if you thought it was perfect at the beginning, looking back at it in the future, it may still be wrong.

如果大家同意这个观点，就不要再纠结自己生活中犯下的错误，哪怕是严重的错误。未来永远是全新的，把错误总结出来，当成自己的财富。在未来就有可能避免这些错误的发生，使自己更加优秀。一味地纠结、后悔对生活是没有一点帮助的。

If everyone agrees with this point of view, stop worrying about the mistakes you have made in your life, even serious mistakes. The future is always brand new, if you sum up the mistakes as your own wealth. In the future it is possible to avoid these mistakes and make yourself better. Blind entanglement and regret will not help life at all.

我们再来读几个小故事。

第一个是卖瓷碗的老人。一个卖瓷碗的老人挑着扁担在路上走着，突然一个瓷碗掉到地上摔碎了，但是老人头也不回继续向前走。

路人看到很奇怪，便问："为什么你的碗摔碎了，你不生气，看都不看一下呢？"

老人答道："我再怎么回头看，碗都是碎的。难道我生气，看一下它，碗就会复原吗？"

Let's read a few more stories.

The first is an old man who sells porcelain bowls. An old man selling porcelain bowls was walking on the road carrying a pole when suddenly a porcelain bowl fell to the ground and shattered, but the old man didn't turn his head and continued to move forward.

When passersby saw it very strange, they asked, "Why did your bowl shatter, you are not angry, and you don't even look at it?"

The old man replied, "No matter how I look back, the bowls are all broken. Am I angry, if I look at it, will the bowls recover?"

失去的东西就要学着去接受，学着放下。毕竟很多事并不会因为你的悲伤就会回来，结果就会被改变。

You have to learn to accept what you have lost, and learn to let go. Because many things will not get better because of your grief, nor will it change the results that have been formed.

第二个是烧水的故事。师父问："如果你要烧壶开水，

生火到一半时发现柴不够，你该怎么办？"有的弟子说赶快去找，有的说去借，有的说去买。师父说："为什么不把壶里的水倒掉一些呢？"世事总不能万般如意，有舍才有得。

The second is the story of boiling water. The master asked, "If you want to boil a pot of boiling water and find that there is not enough firewood in the middle of the fire, what should you do?" Some disciples say hurry up to find it, some say borrow it, some say buy it. The master said, "Why don't you dump some of the water in the pot?" Things can't always go as they please, only if you give up. Learn to let go before you can get it.

第三个是猴子的执着。在亚洲，有一种捉猴子的陷阱。他们把椰子挖空，然后用绳子绑起来，接在树上或固定在地上。椰子上留了一个小洞，洞里放了一些食物，洞口大小恰好只能让猴子空着手伸进去，而无法握着拳头伸出来。当猴子闻香而来，它将手伸进去抓食物，理所当然地，紧握的拳头便缩不出洞口。当猎人来时，猴子惊慌失措，也不肯松手，更是逃不掉。没有任何人捉住猴子不放，它是

被自己的执着所俘虏，它只需将手放开就能缩回来。

The third is the monkey's persistence. In Asia, there is a trap for catching monkeys. They hollowed out the coconuts and tied them with ropes, attached to trees or fastened to the ground. There was a small hole in the coconut, and some food was put in the hole. The hole was just the size for the monkey to stick in with its bare hands, but not with a clenched fist. When the monkey smells the fragrance, its hand will reach in to grab the food, and at this time, the clenched fist will not be able to retract the hole. When the hunter arrived, the monkey panicked and refused . Of course, it couldn't escape. No one holds the monkey, it is captured by its own clinging. It just needs to let go of its hands and it can retract. Desires in our hearts make us unable to let go of our inner desires and attachments, and keep us bound. The only thing we have to do is to open our hands, let go of unnecessary attachments, and be free and easy.

有时候，自己很想要的东西如果要不到，我们要学会放弃，最后的结果可能会让我们意想不到。

Sometimes, if we can't get what we really want, we have to learn to give up, and the final result may surprise us.

1. 放下面子

我们低头，是为了看准脚下的路，搞清楚你到底需要什么，不要输在虚无的面子上。

1. Put down

We bow our heads in order to see the road under our feet, to find out what you need, and not to lose the face of nothingness.

2. 放下压力

累与不累，取决于自己的心态。心灵的房间，把一些无谓的痛苦都丢掉，才能给快乐腾出些空间。

2. Let go of the pressure

Tired or not, it depends on your state of mind. The room of the soul, should throw away some unnecessary pain, in order to make some space for happiness.

3. 放下过去

既然已成定局，学会理智地接受现实，毕竟再做什么也无法挽回。活在当下，把握当下。

3. Let go of the past

Now that it is a foregone conclusion, learn to accept the reality rationally. After all, nothing can be done to restore it. Live in the moment, seize the moment.

4. 放下自卑

不是每个人都可以成为伟人，但每个人都可以成为内心强大的人。相信自己，别人可以做到的，你同样不差。

4. Let go of your inferiority complex

Not everyone can be great, but everyone can be strong at heart. Believe in yourself, if others can do it, you are not bad either.

5. 放下懒惰

把一件平凡的小事做到炉火纯青，就是绝活。集中一点，做到最好。

5. Let go of laziness

To make an ordinary little thing perfect is a unique skill. Concentrate a little and do your best.

6. 放下消极

只要你愿意，你完全可以一辈子都做最好的自己。没有谁能够左右胜负，除了你。自己的战争，你就是最优秀的将军！

6. Let go of negativity

You can be your best self for the rest of your life if you want. No one can control the outcome, except you. In your own war, you are the best general!

7. 放下抱怨

与其抱怨，不如努力。现在所有的困难，都是为以后的成功做准备。

7. Let go of complaining

Instead of complaining, work hard. All the difficulties now are to prepare for future success.

8. 放下犹豫

不要优柔寡断，选准了一个方向，就只管上路，不要回头。如果你有什么好的想法，那就立即行动吧，不让自己后悔。

8. Let go of hesitation

Don't be indecisive, choose a direction, just go on the road, don't look back. If you have a good idea, do it now and don't let yourself regret it.

9. 放下狭隘

宽容是一种美德，宽容别人，其实也是给自己的心灵让路。只有在宽容的世界里，人才能奏出和谐的生命之歌！

9. Let go of narrowness

Tolerance is a virtue. Tolerance to others is actually giving way to one's own soul. Only in a tolerant world can people play a harmonious song of life!

10. 放下怀疑

心存疑虑，做事难成。要成功，头脑简单向前冲！

10. Let go of doubt

Always doubt everything, it's hard to do one thing. To succeed, keep your mind simple and rush forward!

向 前
Move Forward

我们还是先来读两个小故事吧。

Let's start with two short stories.

1858 年，瑞典一个富人家生下了一个女儿，然而不久，女孩就染上了一种无法解释的瘫痪症，丧失了走路的能力。一次，一家人乘船去旅行。船长的太太给女孩讲，船长有一只天堂鸟，它是如此的美丽，女孩被船长太太的描述迷住了，极想亲自看一看。于是保姆带着女孩来到甲板，让女孩在那里等她，她自己先去找船长。

In 1858, a wealthy family in Sweden gave birth to a daughter, but soon the girl contracted an unexplained paralysis and lost her ability to walk. Once, the family took a boat trip. The captain's wife told the girl that the captain had a bird of paradise, which was so beautiful. The girl was fascinated by the description of the captain's wife and wanted to see it for herself. So the nanny took the girl to the deck and asked the girl to wait for her there, while she went to the captain first.

孩子耐不住性子等待，她要求旁边服务生立即带她去看天堂鸟。而那个服务生并不知道女孩的腿不能走路，就愉快地答应了，服务生只顾着带着她一道去看那只美丽的鸟。这时，奇迹发生了，女孩因为过度的渴望，竟忘我地拉住了服务生的手，慢慢地走了起来。从此，孩子的病便痊愈了。女孩长大以后，又忘我地投入到文学创作中，最后成了第一位荣获诺贝尔文学奖的女性，她就是茜尔玛·拉格萝芙。

The child couldn't bear to wait, she asked the waiter next to her to take her to see the bird of paradise immediately. And the waiter didn't know that the girl's legs couldn't walk, so he happily agreed, the waiter only took her to see the beautiful bird. At this time, a miracle happened. The girl lost

herself because of her excessive desire. She grabbed the waiter's hand and walked slowly. Since then, the child's illness has been cured. When the girl grew up, she devoted herself to literary creation, and finally became the first woman to win the Nobel Prize for Literature. She is Thelma Lagrove.

"忘我"是走向成功的一条捷径，在这种环境中，人往往才会超越自身的束缚，释放出无限的潜能。

"Forgetting oneself" is a shortcut to success. In this environment, people often transcend their own constraints and release unlimited potential.

有师徒两位僧人，从很远的地方去灵山朝圣。一路上一边乞食一边赶路，日夜兼程，不敢稍有停息。因为在行前，他们发了誓愿，要在佛诞日那天赶到圣地。作为僧人，最重要的就是守信、虔诚、不妄语，何况是对佛陀发的誓愿呢！

There were two monks, master and apprentice, who went on a pilgrimage to Lingshan from far away. Along the way, they hurry along while begging for food, traveling day and night, daring not stop for a while. Because before the trip, they made a vow to arrive at the holy place on the Buddha's birthday. As a monk, the most important thing is to be faithful, pious, and not to lie, not to mention the vows made to the Buddha!

但在穿越一片沙漠时，年轻的弟子却病倒了。这时离佛诞日已经很近了，而他们距灵山的路还有很远。为了完成誓愿，师父开始搀扶着弟子走，后来又背着弟子走。这样一来，行进的速度就慢了许多，三天只能走完原来一天的路程。

But while crossing a desert, the young disciple fell ill. At this time, it was very close to the Buddha's birthday, and they were still far from the road to Lingshan. In order to fulfill the vow, the master started to walk with the disciples, and later walked with the disciples on his back. As a result, the speed of the journey was much slower, and the original one-day distance could only be covered in three days.

到了第五天，弟子已经气息奄奄，快不行了。他一边

流泪一边央求师父："师父啊，弟子罪孽深重，无法完成向佛陀发下的誓愿了，并且还连累了您，请您独自走吧，不要再管弟子，日程要紧。"师父怜爱地看着弟子，又将他背到背上，边艰难地向前行走边说："徒儿啊，朝圣是我们的誓愿，灵山是我们的目标。既然已经上路，已经在走，灵山就在心中，佛陀就在眼前了。佛绝不会责怪虔诚的人，让我们能走多远走多远吧……"

On the fifth day, the disciple was dying. While crying, he begged the master, "Master, the disciple has sinned so much that I can't fulfill the vow we made to the Buddha, and I has also affected you. Please go alone, don't worry about me, the schedule is important." The master looked at it lovingly. Looking at his disciple, he carried him to his back again, and while walking forward with difficulty, he said, "pilgrimage is our vow, and Lingshan is our goal. Since we have already set out on the road and are walking, Lingshan is in our hearts. The Buddha is at hand. The Buddha will never blame the devout. Let us go as far as we can..."

其实，每个人都有自己的目标和誓愿，每个人都是朝圣者。由于各种客观和主观的原因，并非每个人都能达到目标和实现誓愿。尽管每个人的目标和誓愿都不相同，只要你上了路，向目标靠近，你就已经到达了，因为每个人的灵山都不一样。关键是你要整装上路，要向前走！能走多远走多远……

In fact, everyone has their own goals and vows, and everyone is a pilgrim. For various objective and subjective reasons, not everyone can reach their goals and fulfill their vows. Although everyone's goals and vows are different, as long as you get on the road and get closer to the goal, you have already arrived, because everyone's spiritual mountain is different. The key is that you have to pack up and move forward! You can go as far as you can…

人的每一天，都可以看作是自己生命的一个全新的开始。如同我们出去旅行，出去攀登，风景总是在前方等着我们。

Every day of a person can be regarded as a new beginning of his life. Like when we go out to travel, or go out to climb, the scenery is always waiting for us ahead.

如果你对自己现在不满意，对过去不满意，我们完全可以尝试着不管或者忘记过去，让崭新的自己去迎接美好新的一天。如果今天做的还不对，或者是还不够好、不满意，那么，我们明天就重新开始，多做几次，不断重复。这样，我们的人生就有了无限的可能，有了无限的期待，就和万花筒一样色彩缤纷。

If you are not satisfied with yourself now and with the past, we can try to ignore or forget the past, and let the new self welcome a better new day. If what we do today is not right, or not good enough, and not satisfied, then we can start over tomorrow, do it a few more times, and repeat. In this way, our life has infinite possibilities and infinite expectations, which is as colorful as a kaleidoscope.

远方有爱情在等着你，未来有财富在等着你，明天有

新的朋友在等着你，前方有你从未看过的风景在等着你。

Love is waiting for you in the distance, wealth is waiting for you in the future, new friends are waiting for you tomorrow, and scenery that you have never seen before is waiting for you.

快乐、尖叫、幸福、激情、温馨、荣耀都在未来召唤你，只要生命尚存，这些都是属于你的！在新的黎明醒来，整理好心情，出发吧！

Joy, screaming, happiness, passion, warmth, glory, all are calling you in the future. As long as life exists, these are all yours! Wake up in the new dawn, pack your mood, and go!

未 来
The Future

在浩瀚的宇宙中，人类终将会寻找、创造出一片乐土。

In the vast universe, human beings will eventually find and create a land of happiness and joy.

在这片土地上，没有疾病，人们健康地生活。

In this land, there is no disease and people live a healthy life.

在这片土地上，废除了货币，人们不会为金钱奔波，更不会因为金钱而违反道德、出卖灵魂。人们按照需要分配着工作，供应着精美的食物和用品。

In this land, currency is abolished. People will not run around for money, nor will they violate morality and sell their souls because of money. People are assigned jobs as needed, and fine food and

supplies are provided.

在这片土地上，消除了阶层和特权，自由的思想深入人心，每个人都是一个神圣的个体，爱是人相互交流的基础。

In this land, classes and privileges are eliminated, the idea of freedom is deeply rooted in the hearts of the people, everyone is a sacred individual, and love is the basis of human communication.

同时，我们向往的社会礼仪、规范已经成为了人类自觉遵守的习惯。我们随心在星际之间旅游探险，和星际中的其它物种和睦相处，礼尚往来，互通有无。

At the same time, the social etiquette and norms we yearn for have become habits that humans consciously abide by. We travel and explore the interstellar space at will, and live in harmony with other species in the interstellar space.

科技的发达，已经不需要我们再去了解过去，因为我们与生俱来就掌握了宇宙中已有的知识和道理，人们唯一可以做的就是不断地发现和探索，并要求专业的部门更新

我们的知识库。

The development of science and technology no longer requires us to understand the past, because we are born with the knowledge and truth in the universe. The only thing people can do is to constantly discover and explore, and ask professional departments to update our knowledge base.

我们终于拥有了征服自然的能力，熟练地掌握了宇宙的运行规律，学会了利用宇宙中最强大的能量。

We finally have the ability to conquer nature, master the laws of the universe, and learn to use the most powerful energy in the universe.

在未来，我们虽然相对于宇宙还是那么渺小，如同一粒细小的尘埃。但是，我们和其它星辰一样，构织着神奇绚丽的宇宙。人类和自然融为一体，在那里闪耀着自己的光芒。至此，我们不再是宇宙的索取和破坏者，而是贡献者。

In the future, we will still be so small relative to the universe, like a tiny speck of dust. However, like other stars, we make up a magical and gorgeous universe. Humans and nature merge into one, where they shine with their own light. At this point, we are no longer the taker and destroyer of the universe, but the contributor.

人与人之间，人与其它生物之间，人与宇宙之间，是和谐，是共存。

Between people, between people and other creatures, between people and the universe, there is harmony and coexistence.